I0829473

THE NAUGHTY AND *nice* BOOK OF CHRISTMAS PUNS

CHRISTMAS PUNS FOR THE MOST PUNDERFUL TIME OF THE YEAR

TREE-REX

IT'S CHRISTMAS,
ALPACA GIFT!

CHRISTMAS
QUACKER

♪O HOLEY KNIGHT♪

LET'S TACO 'BOUT
CHRISTMAS

HOW RUDE-OLPH
YOU...

YOU'VE GOT BALLS COMING DRESSED LIKE THAT...

SANTA JAWS

♪ 'TIS THE SEASON
TO BE JELLY ♪

HAVE A BEAR-Y
CHRISTMAS

OH SNAP!

♪ OH CHRISTMAS BEE ♪
OH CHRISTMAS BEE

MERRY
CRUSTMAS!

HAVE A MEOWY
CHRISTMAS

SANTA PAWS

MISTLE-TOAD

AVO MERRY CHRISTMAS, MY OTHER HALF

BAH HUM-PUG

IT'S CHRISTMAS,
DON'T BE A PRICK

♪ SANTA CLAWS IS COMING TO TOWN ♪

WHALE YOU KISS
ME UNDER THE
MISTLETOE?

♪ DACHSHUND THROUGH THE SNOW ♪

I LOVE CHRISTMAS SNOW MUCH!

BUT FIRST,
LET ME TAKE AN ELFIE
#1 ELF

CHRISTMOUSE
TIME IS HERE

HOPPY
HOLIDAYS

IT'S CHRISTMAS!
I'M SO EXCITED, I WET MY PLANTS!

IT'S THE MOST
♪ WINE-DERFUL TIME ♪
OF THE YEAR

I LOVE HANGING
WITH YOU

JINGLE SMELLS
JINGLE SMELLS

ALSO AVAILABLE...

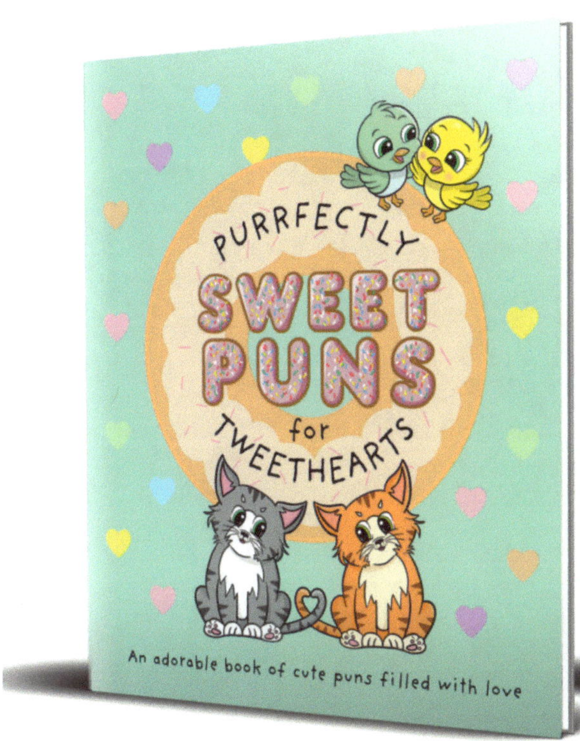

'PURRFECTLY SWEET PUNS FOR TWEETHEARTS'
+
'THE SMART ASS BOOK OF PUNS'

WWW.LEFDDESIGNS.COM

The Naughty and Nice Book of Christmas Puns

© 2020 LEFD Designs

All Rights Reserved.

www.lefddesigns.com